Locked in A Castle

By

Lizzy Stevens

&

Steve Miller

Publisher's Note:
This is a work of fiction. All names, characters, places, and events are the work of the author's imagination.
Any resemblance to real persons, places, or events is coincidental.

Dedication:

This book is dedicated to our two boys!

A note to our readers:

Thanks for reading our books!
You can find Lizzy on Twitter
@Lizzystevens123

Want to make a Difference? Donate to The Epilepsy Foundation. You can find their website here:
https://epilepsyfoundation.secure.force.com/EpilepsyPublicDonationP
Every little bit helps.

Chapter One

Kelly heard a car coming up the long drive and hurried to the window to see who it was. Looking out, she saw her guardian, Jack, coming. For a moment hope ran through her body. "I wonder if he has another man ready to come to the castle? Someone that will free me from this curse."

Kelly Taylor moved through the castle to greet him. It was the same as it'd been every other day since the warlock had cursed her. She was trapped within the boundaries of the castle's grounds, waiting for the one man that could break the curse. Many have come but they were always scared away. A sadness fell over her face when she thought about all the men over the years that were too scared to even talk to her much less fall in love with her so the curse would be broken. She was trapped year after year never able to leave the grounds and never aging. All she could do was hope and pray that one day her guardian would send the right man to her. Knowing that the curse would be broken was all she had to hold onto. Every day she would be in ghost form and every night at midnight she would get her life back and be human but only until morning. Even as human she was trapped to the confines of the grounds never able to leave until the curse was broken.

She slowly made it through the great hall and past the white ivory fireplace that Jack always kept going. Along the walls were paintings of all of her ancestors. She didn't know much about them but never felt like it was right to remove the photos. Kelly drifted into the room to wait for Jack.

Jack was an immortal shape shifter. He had been with her since the beginning. He was like a father to her. As the years passed, he shifted into a new face so the town's people never questioned why he never aged.

She waited patiently as Jack parked the car and walked into the castle then met him at the front door.

Jack smiled as he saw her. "Good morning, Kelly. I do have some good news for you."

Kelly smiled back at him. She loved it when Jack had the time to come see her. He was her only friend. "What do you have for me? Or should I say who do you have for me?" She smiled. "I'm guessing there is a new man all ready to come here for me to scare off as soon as he sees my ghost self." The smile faded from her face.

Jack walked over to her. "Don't give up on me Kelly. I think I have found the perfect guy this time. I really do feel like it's going to work. Be strong. Don't let him win."

Kelly put on a fake smile for Jack. She didn't want him disappointed because he had tried so hard over the many years. "I won't give up, Jack. I know it will work. But when it does and I'm finally free I'm going to get my revenge on him."

Jack shook his head and firmly said, "No, you are not. You are going to break this curse and then live a happy life. You are not going to anything other than be happy. Besides, you know he isn't alive anymore. I've told you the story over and over about his death. Just be happy that the curse is broken."

Kelly saw Jack was genuinely worried about her. “Okay you win. I will behave myself. I won’t go after anyone in his family. As long as they don’t come after me. But what I don’t understand is why didn’t it break when he died?” She wondered. “So, tell me. What’s the story on the new guy and when does he get here?”

Jack started to walk into the kitchen. “I’m going to go grab a soda before we get started.”

Kelly followed behind. “This can’t be good if you don’t want to tell me. What is wrong with him? I don’t want to waste my time if there isn’t a chance of him being the one.”

Jack got a soda from the refrigerator and popped the top. “Kelly, we don’t know what is going to happen until the guy gets here and we let it all play out.”

She walked closer. “Okay but what are you not telling me about him? I can tell when you are hiding something.”

Jack looked at her and with hesitation said. “Okay, here it goes. This one is a not going to be super easy. I wanted to make sure this time that the guy would not get scared off and run."

Kelly interrupted. "Yeah, and how exactly did you make sure of this?"

Jack sipped his soda. "Hear me out. I found a great guy. I decided I would get somebody who would be more able to handle that you are a ghost. So, I turned to only looking for somebody who was a witch or shapeshifter. This way he would have something in common with both of us. I had a stack of witches to interview for the position. I didn't break any of the conditions. I didn't tell him there is a ghost here and I didn't tell him that you are a witch. We didn't break any 'rules'. When I finally decided on the guy, I had him sign a contract saying that he would be awarded one million dollars if he was able to stay here at the castle for a full year. The stipulation of the contract says he is only allowed to leave for an hour a day to run errands and get groceries. Anything he needs to do he can go do but can't be gone more than an hour."

Kelly started pacing back and forth. "So, you are keeping him trapped here with me?"

Jack walked over to the table and set his soda can down. "I'm not really trapping the guy. I'm simply giving him an incentive to stay. All the other guys were scared off when they found out you were a ghost and they never got to know the real you. This time I'm making it possible for him to get to know you."

Kelly rubbed her forehead. "I don't know how he is supposed to fall in love with me if he's only here for the money."

Jack smiled. "Oh, but my dear, that is where you come into it. He won't be able to not fall in love with you once he gets to know you."

Kelly loved the way Jack always took care of her. It really didn't surprise her that he would go to these lengths to try and save her. He was an amazing guardian and once her curse was broken the council would find him another witch to be the care giver for.

"When can I expect him?" She asked.

Jack started to walk to the door. “He will be here first thing in the morning.”

“What did you tell him about me?”

Jack looked up at her with caring eyes and a smile. “Don’t worry, Kelly. I wouldn’t have sent somebody if I didn’t think they had a chance. I told him that a wonderful woman lived in the castle too that he might run into from time to time. The rest he will learn in time.”

Kelly wasn’t sure that she completely liked the idea but at this point it’s worth giving it a try. “Okay thanks. All I can do is see what happens. Until tomorrow.” She said as she walked Jack to the door.

Chapter Two

Kelly nervously floated around. She would be meeting her possible new love that day. As she paced back and forth her head was full of so many thoughts. "Maybe I'll wait until tonight to introduce myself so he's not greeted by a ghost. Yes, that's what I'll do. I'll keep my ghost form a secret for a little bit." She paced back and forth. "Okay I've lost my mind. I'm talking to myself now."

As she heard the car pulling down the drive, she hurried up the stairs to the attic. She wanted to watch through the window as he made his way into her life. She watched as a blue full-size four-wheel drive Chevy truck pulled in front of the house. She wasn't sure what year it was. Being locked in the castle for so many years all the years were starting to run together and the least of her worries was keeping up with the latest new car report. She watched as he got out and grabbed two suitcases from the back of the truck.

She heard the front door open and a voice say. “Hello. Is anyone home? Jack said that he let you know I would be arriving today. My name is Dane.”

Kelly listened but didn’t say a word. She planned to wait until midnight to make a sound. It would be easier than jumping out and saying boo. She stayed in the attic all day waiting until nightfall. When it finally arrived, her body was filled with nerves. It was time to meet the new guy.

She walked down the stairs to the kitchen to fix some food. It was hard to wait all day for food, too. As a ghost she couldn’t eat anything. Not that she felt the hunger but it was an adjustment for her when the curse first started. She was used to doing the normal thing which meant you cooked and ate three meals a day. As she walked through the dinning room, she saw Dane sitting at the solid oak long table reading. He sat there with his back to her. His dark brown almost black hair went to about his shoulders with just a little wave in it.

Dane glanced over his shoulder as he heard a noise. “Hi.” He said. “You must be Kelly. Jack told me that you would probably be working and I wouldn’t see you until late. I wanted to introduce myself since we would be living here together.”

Kelly wasn’t sure what to think. She didn’t know if she would like him or if he would like her. Her nerves were on edge. “Hi. It’s nice to meet you. I do keep crazy hours but I’ll try to be quiet as I wander around the castle late at night.”

Dane smiled. “No don’t go out of your way for me. This is your home and I’m a guest in it. You do everything the way you normally would and pay no attention to me. Most of the time I’ll be working anyway. I work from home on my computer and generally I wear a headset so I probably won’t hear you.”

Kelly nodded with a smile. “I’m going to fix me something to eat. Do you want anything?”

Dane shook his head no. “No, I’m good but thanks.” He said as he lifted his soda. “I just needed a drink.

Kelly nodded and gave him a small smile. "Okay well I'm going to get something and then go for a walk. I'm sure I'll see you around." She didn't want to try too hard too fast. If it was meant to be then it would be. She turned and walked away.

She went into the kitchen and looked around to see what she might want. Jack was great about keeping everything stocked for her since she couldn't leave the grounds. She walked over to the refrigerator and got out the cheese and butter. She thought that a grilled cheese was exactly what she wanted. Kelly grilled up the sandwich and got some chips to go with it and then went to the table to enjoy the few hours she would have before daylight would come again and she would be trapped. A sadness fell over her. The years went by one by one and never a chance of getting out. All she could do was hope that Dane would be that chance that she needed. She hoped that he would break the curse but only time would tell. It had to be true love. It wouldn't work if he fell in love with her but she had no feelings for him. So much was riding on this one guy and he didn't even know. She had gotten used to the routine by now as she had met man after man hoping he would be the one. She tried not to put too much hope into it because she was always disappointed in the end. It was hard though to stay tough and not let herself get carried away in her thoughts.

Kelly finished her food, cleaned up the mess, and then walked outside to her favorite spot. As she walked the concrete walkway into the gardens to sit on the bench she took in a breath. It was more beautiful than before. Jack had a landscaping crew come in and give it a makeover as a surprise for her. The red and white roses that filled the entrance that she walked through took her breath away. She went over and sat on the bench for hours. The time passed faster than she wanted and it was time for her to get back to her room before Dane caught her in her ghost form. Daylight would be upon her soon.

A few hours later Kelly was turned back into a ghost. She was now to float around all day not able to touch anything. It made the day feel as if she was in a prison which was exactly what the warlock who did this wanted. One of the things that was hard to get used to was never sleeping. As a ghost she didn't sleep and as a human she was only up for a few hours so didn't need to sleep. It was, for sure, an odd thing to get used to, but now it had been so many years that it didn't even cross her mind anymore. She went over to the window and watched as Dane walked down the path to the flower garden. "I hate this." She said to an empty room. "I wish I could walk the grounds with him and get to know him."

It wasn't long before she saw Jack driving up the driveway to the house. She wanted to run down the greet him but feared Dane would catch her so she waited in the attic.

Jack parked his truck and walked up to the door of the castle. He came inside and said. "Kelly, I came to see you. Dane is outside so it's all clear."

Kelly yelled down. "Come on up to the attic. I don't want to risk Dane seeing me."

Jack walked in. "I just came to check on you. How was your first night? We only have a few minutes. I saw Dane down by the pond when I drove up."

Kelly smiled. It always made her happy to see Jack. "It was okay. I mean I didn't want to push things so I only had a short conversation with him and then I went out to the garden."

Jack understood. "It sounds like you did everything right. That's what I would have done too. Taking it slow is the way to go." He turned to walk away. "I better get back downstairs before he comes in and wonders why I'm in the attic."

She watched as Jack got in his truck and left unnoticed by Dane. As she floated around, she found that the day would drag on forever. She knew she was going to have to go outside of those walls or it would make her crazy. Kelly went downstairs and out the back so Dane wouldn't see her. She went around the grounds until midnight and then walked back into the house as a real person.

Chapter Three

Kelly started back inside the house not sure if she hoped to run into Dane or that she wouldn't. She walked in and didn't see Dane anywhere and the nerves started to fade a little.

She decided to do the usual and go to the kitchen for some food. When she walked into the kitchen, she saw a covered plate on the counter with a note. Kelly walked over to the note and read,

"Kelly,

I thought you might be hungry when you got in from work. I made you some of my world-famous homemade beef stew. Okay it might not be world famous but it's pretty damn good."

Kelly couldn't help but laugh as she uncovered the dish. It was still warm so he must have left it not long ago. It smelled delicious. She ate it all without a second thought and then washed the dishes. She walked over to the drawer and got a pen and piece of paper. She wanted to leave him a thank you note.

"Dane,

Thanks so much for the stew. It really must be world famous. I thought it was amazing."

Kelly sat the note down with a smile across her face. "Maybe one day we will get to know each other." She thought to herself.

She left the kitchen, picked up her journal and started to the garden. It was her peaceful place. She wanted to write down her thoughts before she forgot. Maybe one day the notes would be helpful in breaking the curse.

As she sat there on the bench looking up at the stars she wondered aloud. "How many more years do I have to be cursed. It's not fair." Tears started to flow from her eyes as she wiped them away with her hand. "Crying isn't going to accomplish anything. Now pull yourself together." She scolded herself. She needed to get back inside to the attic before Dane caught her as a ghost. She hated the attic. All she could do was stay awake for hours on end. It made for a long day at times.

Kelly went over to the table where Jack had been so kind to print out books for her so she could read. As she couldn't touch the pages there would be no way for her to turn them. So, Jack printed them out for her and laid them all in order on the large table so she could enjoy reading books from time to time. Short stories were the best because they wouldn't take up so much time and space. She could read a couple a night and then Jack would change them out for her the next time he came over. It helped pass the time until she was in human form and could walk around and actually touch things.

The day crept along like all the rest. She hid in the attic until nightfall and then she snuck down the stairs as to not run into Dane. She didn't know how she would explain that she had been hanging out in the attic all day. When nightfall came, she went to the kitchen to do what she thought would be the same thing as every other night. But when she walked in, she saw a note on the counter. A smile came across her face. Why? She didn't know. She assumed it was from Dane and that made her smile. She walked over and picked it up.

Hi Kelly,

It's me again. Your friendly neighborhood pen pal. I had a thought. Maybe we could have dinner tomorrow night. I know you work crazy hours. So how about I cook us up a nice meal to be ready at about midnight. If you show up great but if you have to work late, I completely understand. No hard feelings will be had. I promise."

Kelly couldn't help but smile even bigger. She did really want to spend time with Dane. She wrote a note back.

"Midnight sounds perfect. I can't wait. See you then."

She put the note in the usual spot on the counter and then strolled out to the bench that she sat on every night and gazed at the stars.

The next night Kelly was overly excited for her date with Dane. "Okay don't overreact. Take things slow. This is a good step forward." She said to herself. She didn't want to rush things but knew that she did need to at least get the ball rolling or how else would they ever fall in love.

She didn't want to overdress just because they were spending a little time together. Kelly went over to her closet and got a pair of jeans and a nice t-shirt. She was thankful for Jack always making sure her closet was stocked with new clothes. If it wasn't for him all of her stuff would have holes in it from having to wear the same thing every day for all these years. After she got dressed, she went over and brushed her long dark brown hair. She couldn't decide if she wanted to pull it up or leave it down so she ended up doing a half up half down kind of thing. Her hair was out of her face but still flowed down a little on her back too.

She walked down the stairs and into the kitchen where she found Dane doing last minute touches to their dinner.

"Can I help with anything?" Kelly asked.

Dane shook his head. "No. Of course not. I have got this covered. You are about to taste the best lasagna you have ever tasted."

Kelly smiled. "I love lasagna."

Dane gave her a sheepish grin. "I know. I have to admit. I asked Jack what you liked."

Kelly laughed. She couldn't believe he went to all that trouble. "Thanks for this. I'm sure it will be great."

"If you want, you can go ahead and go to the dining room. I'll bring the food out in a couple of minutes. I'm fixing our plates now. I've already set some sweet iced tea on the table. I hope that's okay. Jack said you liked tea."

Kelly smiled. "It's perfect." She walked on into the dining room and waited for Dane to bring their food out.

She watched as Dane carried a tray over to the table and sat it down. Kelly looked down at her plate to see the promised lasagna and garlic bread on the plate and a small bowl with a salad. The salad looked amazing. It was full of romaine lettuce, bacon bits, shredded cheddar cheese, and top with croutons. She saw a bottle of Ranch dressing sitting to the side.

Kelly looked over at Dane. "This looks incredible. You didn't have to go to all of this trouble.

"No trouble at all." Dane said. "I enjoy cooking. I hope you like it. I don't do the traditional lasagna that most people make. I don't like fillers so I don't use cottage cheese or ricotta, but I do add a bell pepper. I love the taste so I hope you do too."

Kelly couldn't wait to try it. She took a bite and the flavors danced around in her mouth. "This is incredible."

Dane smiled. "I'm glad you like it. I was really hoping we would be able to get together tonight. I have been wanting to for a while now but our paths keep crossing."

A sadness fell over Kelly. She hated the way her life was, but she dreamed, hoped and prayed that one day the curse would be broken.

"So, tell me a little bit about yourself, Kelly."

Kelly was a little thrown off by the question because she didn't know what she could and couldn't say. "Well let's see. I have lived in this town my entire life. I've been in this castle for more years than I can even count." She put on a fake smile so he wouldn't think much of the comment.

Dane nodded. “It’s a beautiful place to live. Do you have family here?”

Kelly thought before answering. “Jack. He is the only family I have really.”

“He’s great.” Dane agreed.

They talked for hours. Kelly was having the best time. It had been a while since she had somebody to talk to other than Jack.

Dane glanced at his watch. “Wow! I can’t believe it’s almost morning. We talked all night.”

Kelly started coughing and choking on her drink. She wasn’t expecting the night to have been over. She had to get out of there and fast. She couldn’t risk him seeing her as a ghost.

“Are you okay?” Dane asked.

Kelly sat her drink down. “Oh yeah. It just went down the wrong way.” She smiled. “But I do need to go. I hate to but I have an appointment in less than an hour. I didn’t realize we talked all night. But I’m not complaining. I had a great time and thank you so much for dinner.” She stood up and started to walk away.

Dane stood. “I had a good time too and hope we can do it again soon.”

Kelly was already walking fast to get upstairs and out of sight. She looked over her shoulders. “Yes, we will. I can’t wait.”

Chapter Four

Kelly floated back and forth across the attic floor. How was she supposed to explain why she suddenly ran away? She wasn't sure that her work excuse was going to be believable enough for Dane not to push the issue. She wanted to call Jack and get his thoughts but thought she should give him a break from her problems.

As she floated around the room, she heard Dane leave. She watched as he went down the drive then hurried down the stairs to the back yard. She hated being locked up in the attic all day. The visits from Jack helped her get through the day. As she floated across the grass, she wished she could actually touch the flowers and hold them in her hands. She was lost in her own mind when she was quickly brought out of it.

"What the hell?" Dane said.

Kelly didn't know what to do. The look of shock and fear crossed her mind all at once. She quickly turned and hurried to the attic. She couldn't even try to talk to him right now. "What am I going to do?" She said to herself as she paced back and forth in the attic. "I need Jack." She hurried over to the phone. Even though she couldn't hold it Jack had set it up for voice calling. All she needed to do was say call Jack and the phone would call him.

"Call Jack" She waited impatiently for him to answer.

"What's up Kelly? You never call in the middle of the day. What is going on?"

Kelly hesitated. "Um. Well, what's happened is."

Jack interrupted. "Kelly, just tell me. You are starting to worry me."

"Okay. Dane just saw my ghost form."

The phone went silent for a moment.

"Jack. Are you there?"

"Yes Kel. Just hold on. Don't over react. We will figure this out. I'll be right there."

"Thanks Jack. I love you. You're the best as always."

"Love you too Kel. I'll be right there."

She nervously floated back and forth in the attic hoping that Dane wouldn't come up there. She knew he must be freaked out and probably packing his clothes but she couldn't check. She thought it would be best if she stayed in there until Jack got there.

It wasn't long before she heard Jack pulling in. As she listened for the truck door to close, she got more and more nervous. She floated back and forth thinking it seemed to be taking a really long time for Jack to get to her. Then she heard the big heavy oak door open.

"Kelly! What the hell is going on? Why is Jack here all of the sudden too?"

Kelly was shocked to hear that it was Dane. She was expecting it to be Jack. She didn't know what to say.

"Kelly, I know you are up there. Would you just talk to me please?"

Kelly didn't move. She didn't know what to do. Then she heard Jack. "Kel. I'm here. Don't worry. You can come down. Dane can handle this."

Kelly heard Dane and Jack talking as she came down.

"Handle what?" Dane said. "What the hell is going on?"

Jack held up a hand to Dane. "Just wait. It will all be clear in minutes."

Kelly started floating down the stairs stopping in front of Dane. "I'm sorry. I should have told you."

Dane shook his head back and forth. "Tell me what. I don't understand."

Jack interrupted. "Come sit down and we will explain everything."

The three of them went to the study and Jack fixed Dane a drink.

Dane sipped his vodka and then looked over at Kelly. "Okay now spill. How is this even possible? And don't worry about spooking me. Remember, I am a witch. It's not like I haven't seen odd things before."

Kelly raised her hand out of habit to run it through her hair but in ghost form it was just a wasted effort as her hand wouldn't touch anything. "Okay. I'll just blurt it out as fast as I can because it will be easier for me. Many years ago, I made a warlock mad. He wanted to date me and I wasn't interested. I said no. He said if he couldn't have me then nobody could. He cursed me. I am a ghost all day locked in this castle and then at night I get my human form back but I'm not allowed to leave the castle grounds. He wanted to ensure that I would never meet anyone. I have Jack. He is basically my guardian and takes care of me. He makes sure the house is always stocked with food and the essentials since I can't leave."

Dane sat there in amazement. "That is horrible. I can't believe you have had to live this kind of life. I feel so sorry for you. Have you tried breaking the curse?"

Kelly glanced at Jack and back to Dane. She knew she couldn't tell him the rules of the curse or it wouldn't be broken so she chose her words carefully. "Yes. We have tried. We have researched many potions. None ever work."

Dane still looking somewhat confused said. "Okay so you have this unbreakable curse why bring me here? You obviously didn't want anyone to know about this or you wouldn't hide from me every day. So why am I here? And why offer me the money if I stay a full year?"

Jack jumped in on this question. "Easy. I love Kelly and would do anything for her. She gets lonely. I wanted her to have a friend. Even if was just for a short while. There have been others here but they always get scared off when they see her in her ghost form. That's why this time I gave an incentive to get you to stay longer than a few days. But now that you know you are free to go. You don't have to stay a year. I'll compensate you for your time."

Dane could barely believe all of it. It was all happening so fast. "No. I don't want to leave. I really, truly, do like you, Kelly. I don't mind staying and keeping you company until you get tired of me that is." He said with a laugh.

Kelly could feel her emotions building up. She would be crying a river if her ghost form would let her. She couldn't believe that he wanted to stay.

"And Jack." Dane said. "I don't want the money. I would never dream of accepting payment for hanging out with a great woman."

That made Kelly even more emotional. What would they do next was the question running through her mind as they decided to call it a night.

Chapter Five

The previous night was running laps in Kelly's head. So much had happened. "Does Dane think of me as a friend or more than that? Why is he staying? Okay I really need to stop talking to myself." She said aloud. "I need Jack."

Kelly went over to her voice activated phone and said, "Call Jack."

"Kel, I know we have a small glitch."

Kelly floated back and forth in a not very happy manner. "Jack. A small glitch. Really? He thinks he can research curses and find a fast fix. We can't tell him the cure or the curse won't be broken and he isn't going to find a way to break it in his books. This is all a big waste of time."

There was a pause. "Kel, I know but there is good in all of this."

"What? This is a disaster."

Jack tried to comfort her. "Yes, it is a little bit off track but the good in all of this is Dane wants to stay. He knows the truth about you being a ghost part of the time and he is fine with that. He wants to stay. So, in all of this you have a friend to talk to other than just me. So, there is good in this.

Kelly couldn't disagree. "Thanks, Jack, for everything. I'll let you get back to your day. Love you."

"Love you too Kel and this will all work out."

Kelly heard the phone hang up. She wasn't entirely sure what she was supposed to do. Should she go downstairs to talk to Dane or should she let it sit for a little bit? The thoughts ran wild in her head. If she wasn't in ghost form at the moment, she knew that her head would be pounding.

Moments later Kelly heard a knock at the door.

"Kelly. Are you in there? Can we talk?"

She didn't know if she should say yes or no. It would be awkward either way. "Yes, come in." She ended up saying.

Dane walked in and glanced around. "This place is amazing. It's like going back in time. I love the old Victrola in the corner.

My grandparents had one when I was a kid."

"Thanks." Kelly said. "Jack has done a great job on this place over the years. He puts a lot of time and thought into everything."

Dane nodded. "Huh. I'm not really sure what to say." He smiled. "Is there anyway we could go for a walk and talk?" The minute he said walk he started to try and fix it. "I mean. Um. I didn't mean to..."

Kelly stepped in. "Dane it's fine. I understand. You walk. I'll float." She chuckled. "But yes, I would be happy to spend time with you."

They walked out to the garden and around the fountain.

Dane looked up with a smile. "Hey I have a coin. Have you tried tossing one in the fountain and making a wish?"

Kelly laughed. "You know. I have never tried that. It just might work." She was joking because she knew there was only one way to break the curse and felt like she would never be able to. She did find a good friend in Dane but friendship wasn't going to break the curse.

Dane wanting to continue the fun. grabbed a quarter from his pocket and tossed it in. "Okay. We wish the curse would be broken."

When it of course did not break Kelly laughed. "Well, we tried." She could see how hard he was trying to give her a few minutes of joy.

Dane laughed and then the smile faded. "I'm going to help you with this. I'll research day and night until we find a way to break it."

The smile left Kelly's face. She couldn't let him waste his time. "Dane. I know how to break it. It's not easy."

Shock crossed his face. "Well, what is it. I will help you."

She would cry if she was in human form. Her heart was breaking. "I can't tell you."

"Why not? I can help." He almost shouted.

"I wish I could. But I can't. It's part of the curse. If I tell anyone the way to break it then it can never be broken."

He ran his hands through his hair then looked over at her. "What about Jack? How does he know?"

Kelly floated a little closer to him. "He was there the day the warlock cursed me. He begged him not to. He even offered his own life in my place."

Dane shook his head back and forth. "Wow. I'm so sorry for you, but I'm not giving up. You can't tell me, but I can figure it out on my own and I will."

Kelly tried not to be discouraging because she didn't want to run him off. She needed him there. She needed the company. Life had been lonely and it had been so much better with him there. She smiled. "I'm sure you will figure out."

They spent the next few hours talking and getting to know each other a little better. The day seemed to fly by because before she knew it was nighttime. The sun was setting and the moon was shining. She felt herself starting to change.

Dane watched in awe as her formation happened. "That was incredible." He said. "I mean I know it was probably weird for you and all that. I'm just saying to sit back and watch was something I will never forget. I'm glad you let me in and shared that with me."

Kelly blushed a little as she looked away as to not make eye contact with him. "I'm glad you were here. It's nice to have somebody other than Jack to talk to. I love Jack to death. He is like a father to me. So, I don't want it to come across as bad. I don't mean that at all. I'm just saying it was nice to have you here."

Dane reached out and took her hand. "Do you need to sleep now? I don't know how this works. Are you a ghost all day and then you sleep doing the night? I don't want to keep you from your routine."

She knew that he meant well but she didn't want their time to end. "No. I'm okay, but if you need to go get some sleep I understand."

Dane pulled her closer to him. "No. I'm good. Now that you are back to human form I would love to talk more. We can go in and eat if you want. I will even cook." He said with a smile.

"You always cook." Kelly said. "But it's probably best. I'm not the greatest cook." She laughed.

He took her hand and led her to the house. "It's settled then. I'll fix us something to eat."

They walked back to the house together and into the kitchen. Kelly walked over and sat down at the island counter in the middle of the room while Dane went to the refrigerator to start getting out everything he needed.

He turned to Kelly and said, "I am going to make you the best sandwich you have ever had."

She laughed. "Oh yeah? What's so great about yours? I eat a lot of them. It's the downfall of not being that great of a cook. They are fast and easy."

Dane gave her one of those just wait looks. He got out the sliced sourdough bread first. He buttered it and then set it on the grill pan. Then he got out the ham and cheddar cheese. He built his sandwich and then grilled it on the pan.

Kelly watched from her seat thinking it did look really good. She normally just took some bread from the pack and cold meats and ate the sandwich. She couldn't wait to eat his. It already looked better than what she normally did.

He turned to her. "Your mouth is watering. Isn't it?"

She laughed. "I'll admit it is a step up from the sandwiches that I normally make myself. I can't wait to try it."

It wasn't long before he had them on plates with some chips to go with it. He walked over and sat her plate down in front of her. "Here you go. Your fancy meal."

She laughed as she picked up her grilled ham and cheese to take a bite. She took a bite and nodded her head in approval. "This is really good. Thanks again for cooking for me. You seem to end up doing that a lot."

"I really don't mind. I like to cook. I did kind of want to have a restaurant one day but just never had the money to do it."

Kelly got a serious look for a minute. "Well if you stay for a year Jack will give you the money to do it."

The smile left his face. "Kelly. I told you I'm not taking his money. I want to help. I'm not going anywhere. I'm not leaving you. I will have a restaurant one day after your curse is broken. It might even be something you would want to do with me."

She couldn't help but laugh. "Did you not hear me say that I couldn't cook?"

He smiled. "Yes, I heard you, but there is a lot more to do at a restaurant than just cook. There is the hostess that greets the people and seats them. There is waitresses or waiters who take the orders. Somebody has to bring the food to the people. There is so much more to a restaurant than just a cook. I would love it if you did it with me."

Kelly wasn't really sure how to answer. "Well let's wait and see if we can get the curse broke before we make too many plans for the future."

They talked for a few hours about their plans for the future. Kelly wasn't sure how she felt about that because he never really said anything about them as a couple so she thought maybe they were still just friends. The curse would never be broken that way. She knew she couldn't push it. True love had to come on its own. She called it a night because she didn't want him too tired from staying up all night. It wouldn't bother her because she would be back to a ghost and wouldn't feel it.

Chapter Six

The next morning Kelly started her day like all the rest. Her ghost form arrived right on time and she floated around the room. She didn't want to go downstairs right away and appear to be pushy. She didn't want to be throwing herself on Dane. This was going to have to go at a slow pace even if she was overly impatient with even the glimmer of a chance of breaking the curse. She thought maybe she would talk to Jack and see if he would want to come over for a while and get to know Dane a little better.

"Call Jack." She said to her voice activated phone.

"How's it going, Kel?"

"It's going good. I think. We had a nice night."

Jack interrupted. "Okay but he doesn't just have to fall in love with you. You also have to fall in love with him. It is true love's kiss. Not a one-sided kiss. So, the question is do you have any feelings for him because if not we need to find somebody else. And I'm not asking if you love him. It's too soon. I'm saying is there a spark?"

Kelly waited a minute to answer as she gave it some thought. "I do think there is a spark." She finally said. "I know it won't happen overnight. We need time to get to know each other and let our hearts actually love, but I do feel good about him. He's nothing like any of the others."

"Good" Jack said.

Kelly wanted to ask before he hung up. "Jack, would you want to come over sometime and I don't know have a drink or snack or something so you can get to know him? I know it's a little hard to ask you to dinner as late as it is when I am able to eat. But we could just have a drink or something."

Jack didn't hesitate. "Of course. I wouldn't miss it. How about this weekend?"

"Perfect." She said.

After she hung up, she decided that she needed to go downstairs and see Dane. She couldn't avoid him. They needed to get to know each other if they were ever going to fall in love.

As she floated down the stairs, she heard Dane in the kitchen. She made her way to him.

Dane looked up when she came in. “Hi. I’m making me some lunch.” He hesitated as he looked up at her. “Should I not? I mean is that weird to watch me eat in front of you? I can wait for another time to eat.”

Kelly stopped him. “No. Of course not. You should eat. I get all my eating done after midnight. Don’t feel bad at all. You need to eat.”

Dane hadn’t fixed anything fancy. He was having a fast, quick lunch. A turkey sandwich with cheese was what he had decided on. As he finished making it and sat it on the plate he looked over at Kelly. “Do you want to talk? I can take my sandwich with me if you want to stroll around or we can stay in. Whatever you prefer.”

Kelly liked the idea of spending time with Dane. “Sure. We can go outside. I hate being all locked up inside. I was actually happy when you saw me and wasn't scared away."

Kelly waited for Dane to get his sandwich and a drink and then they went outside. She could see the trees lightly blowing in the breeze and wished she could feel it on her face.

Dane took a bite of his sandwich and then asked. "I don't mean to pry so if you don't want to talk about it you don't have to. Just tell me." He turned and sat down on the bench in front of the water fountain. "But what happened to make the warlock cast this spell. All Jack said was that you wouldn't date the guy and he got mad. I feel like I'm missing something."

Kelly moved back and forth slowly in front of him. "Well there is a little more. The warlock that did this wanted to join powers with me. He said that my family's powers were strong and his was strong so if the two of us joined our powers we would be unstoppable. But I didn't want to cross over to the dark side. I didn't want to be unstoppable. I said no. I wasn't interested. He said if he couldn't have me then nobody could." Kelly paced or floated back and forth and spoke faster as she tried to get it all out. "I said that he couldn't do that. It wasn't fair. So, he said okay I'll give you one way out, but you can never tell anyone how to break the curse or the curse will never be broken. So, I do have one way out but it's pretty much impossible."

Dane sat there trying to wrap his head around everything he just heard. "Oh Kelly. I'm sorry you have had to go through all this. I will find the cure one day. I don't know when but I'm not giving up until I do. That is the promise I'm making to you."

A sadness fell over her. "Don't make promises that you might not be able to keep." She said.

"I'm keeping this one. I have no doubts. Have faith in me. You'll see."

Kelly knew she couldn't say anything. Since she wasn't allowed to say much. You can't very well tell somebody that they have to fall in love with you. You can't make love happen. All she could do was wait and see where things went with Dane. She didn't want to get too overly confident. Jack had invited so many men to her house over the years. They would take one look at her ghost form and run. She didn't blame them. That was a lot to take in. None of them stayed past a couple of days. They didn't get close enough to even get to know her much less fall in love with her. She did feel better about everything so far. Dane knew everything that he could anyway and he still wanted to stay. Maybe the curse could be broken. She wished more than anything that it would be.

Chapter Seven

Six months had gone by with Dane working non-stop every day reading through every spell book he could get his hands on. He made potion after potion and found no cure. Kelly felt horrible that she couldn't just tell him, but she couldn't risk the chance that the warlock didn't actually put that clause in the curse and she had fallen in love with him over the months. She didn't know how he felt about her and wouldn't push it, but she knew how she felt.

It was morning and she had returned to ghost form. She floated down the stairs to see if she could find Dane and she did. She found him in the kitchen making himself some breakfast.

"Good morning." She said.

Dane looked up with a tired look on his face. "Morning." He said with a yawn.

"Are you okay?" Kelly asked.

"Yeah. Just tired. I stayed up all night reading through this new book I got yesterday."

She floated over toward the counter. "I wish you wouldn't kill yourself. You need rest."

He nodded. "I know. I'm not overdoing it." He put his scrambled eggs with cheese on the plate with his bagel that had crème cheese on it. "I was thinking." He said.

"About what?" Kelly asked.

"About the attic. I know all about your ghost form so you don't have to hide out in the attic. You can stay down here with me if you want. I would like it if you were around more."

Kelly was somewhat shocked. She hadn't even thought about it. It would be nice to not feel like she was locked up all the time. "Okay. That sounds good. Tonight, when I'm back to human I'll work on one the rooms."

The day was like all the rest. Dane went over spell after spell and Kelly would make up reason why that one wouldn't work. Things like her and Jack had already tried it.

At night fall when Kelly was back into human form, she walked out to the garden to sit by the fountain. A sadness fell over her. So many years had gone by with the horrible curse. She didn't know how much more she could take. Tears started to fall.

Dane walked up at that very moment. "Are you okay? What can I do? Are you hurt?"

Kelly wiped at the tears. "I'm okay. Just a long day, week, year. Things are just getting to me."

Dane sat down beside her. He pushed her hair out of her face and wiped the tears from her face. "Kel, I promise you that I will find a cure. I'll call some people and see if I can get some help. I'm not going to stop until it's broken."

Kelly sighed. "You can't keep doing this. It's not fair to you. You have already invested close to a year. You should move on and open that restaurant you talked about."

He looked over at her softly. "I'm not going anywhere without you." He said and then he slowly leaned in and kissed her gently on the lips.

Red, blue, pink and green lines of color swirled around her. She felt like she was spinning in circles and maybe she was.

"What is going on?" Dane jumped up and almost yelled.

Kelly stopped after a minute or two. The curse had been broken. She knew deep down that Dane loved her even if he hadn't said it yet. The curse wouldn't have broken if he didn't.

She hurried closer to him. "The curse is broken. You did it."

Dan scratched his head. "I didn't do anything."

Kelly smiled. "You did everything."

"I don't understand. I'm sorry to appear stupid or lost but I don't know what I did. You are going to have to explain."

She took a deep breath. How was she supposed to tell him that he loved her? "Okay to break the curse it had to be done with true love's kiss. I wasn't allowed to tell anyone how to break it. You had to fall in love with me on your own and kiss me on your own without any help from me. And you did. You do love me."

Dane let out what seemed like a mouthful of air. "Wow he said. True love's kiss. What a jackass that guy was. He used an old cliché for a curse. I mean almost every fairy tale out there has that as the way to end a curse. What a great guy." He said with a chuckle.

Kelly laughed. "Well that jackass has kept me locked up for years. He knew that I couldn't leave the grounds so how could I find true love. But you found me. I love you too by the way." She said with a smile.

Dane pulled her into him and kissed her again. Then he held her for a few minutes before letting go. "Do you want to call Jack?"

Kelly turned towards the castle. Yes. I do. He will be so excited." She ran instead of walked all the way to the phone.

She heard Jack say hello on the other end. "Jack can you come over? It's important."

Jack hesitated. "Are you okay. Did something happen?"

"I'm okay. I just really need you."

"I'll be right there." He said.

She hurried to the kitchen to get a bottle of champagne to put on ice. It was defiantly something to celebrate.

Jack arrived about a half hour later.

"Kelly. Is everything okay. You are scaring me." Jack said as he entered the kitchen where Kelly and Dane were waiting for him.

She ran over and gave him a big hug. "Jack. I have amazing news for you."

"What is it?" He wondered aloud.

"The curse is broken." Kelly blurted out as fast as she could. "Dane broke it. He kissed me and it broke. He loves me. He truly loves me."

She looked over at Dane to see a big smile across his face.

Jack couldn't believe it. His eyes got a little teary. He walked over to Kelly. "Oh Kel. This is amazing. You got your life back. Not only your life but a new one with Dane as well. I'm so happy for you. I love you."

She poured a glass of Champaign for each of them. "Cheers." She said as she lifted her glass to take a drink. "It's time for a new life."

Dane walked over and picked up his glass. "Cheers." He said as he lifted it up before taking a drink. "Here's to a new un locked in a castle life."

The End

Enjoy this free story from Lizzy Stevens and Steve Miller.

Cupid's Mistake

Kylie was one of the best cupids around. She was one of the first to show up at work and one of the last to leave. She loved to make the perfect love match. It filled her with joy to see so many people happy.

There were over fifty cupids in Kylie's region. Cupids were always happy and wanted to see other people happy and in love. It was basically in the job description. They brought love to lonely people. Kylie was what you would call a junior cupid still in the training period. She was really good at her job but she was still supervised and watched closely to make sure she didn't make any major mistakes.

When the day was over and Kylie wanted to unwind, she would walk to her favorite restaurant in town. It was always packed full of couples eating romantic meals together. The tables were covered in black tablecloths adorned with white napkins. A bar sat against the back wall with a mirror that covered the full wall. That night was no different than any other night. After work, Kylie walked in and found a seat at the bar.

It wasn't long before she saw a woman sitting alone at a table. The woman looked like she was waiting for somebody. Her hair was fixed nice, she had make up on, she was wearing ear rings and a necklace. It looked as if she had spent some time getting ready for dinner. She noticed her glancing down at her phone several times. A sadness fell over Kylie. She knew that look. The woman was being stood up. She felt bad for her. *I will find her a man that will make her happy. If he can't be here for her then somebody else will be, she thought.* Kylie wasn't supposed to meddle in other people's lives. She was handed assignments and she was to do them. She wasn't supposed to go out on her own and make love connections. *My numbers are the best in the office. Surely I can't get in trouble for this.* she said to herself.

She looked around the restaurant for a single guy who might be the perfect match for her single woman. She was going to make a love connection before the night was over. When she set her mind to something, she usually got what she wanted. She glanced in the mirror of the bar and saw the reflection of the short blond haired woman looking back at her. She pushed her bangs out of her eyes and ordered a soda. She wasn't much of a drinker. As she sipped from her straw, she glanced around the restaurant to see if she could make the perfect love connection.

Kylie saw a guy walk in who looked somewhat lonely. He came in alone and sat down at a small table with nobody with him. *He might be the one,* she thought. He was tall with dark brown hair; wearing a flannel shirt and jeans. She watched him sit down, order a beer and some food, and not really say much to the waitress.

She watched him for a few minutes. Then she looked back over at the sad looking woman. She saw her glancing at her phone again with sad eyes. *It's decided. This is my love connection.* Kylie walked over and touched the woman on the hand and then she walked over and touched the man on the hand. That was all it took. The connection was made. There were no arrows or magical spells needed. All she needed to do was touch them both and the connection was made. She stood back and watched the magic happen.

The woman walked over and immediately started talking to the man. They were both all smiles and they walked out of the restaurant together.

Kylie left the restaurant extremely happy with herself. She walked out almost skipping with the amount of pride in herself. She took it upon herself to jump in and make two people happy. She couldn't wait to tell everyone at work the next day. It didn't take her long to get home. She walked up to the golden gate of the cupid estate where they all shared living quarters. Pink and yellow roses lined both sides of the rock wall fence. Kylie walked through the gate and up to the two story white Victorian style house. It had long white columns on the front porch and a balcony with seats on it for nighttime sitting.

She walked in and up the stairs to her room. Her bedroom had a queen sized bed in the middle of the room, a book shelf full of books in the corner, and a dresser against the back wall. She walked over to the dresser and got out her pajamas before heading to the bathroom to soak in a nice long hot bubble bath.

Kylie started the water and let the vanilla scented bubble bath pour down into the water. Then she stepped into the water and sank down to her shoulders. She stayed in the water until it turned cold before getting out and drying off. It had been a long day and she was getting tired. It wasn't long before she found her way to bed and fell fast asleep.

Kylie walked into work the next day on top of the world. She knew her boss was going to be very happy with her. She walked in and right to the break room. Head Cupid always had breakfast waiting for them so they could get a good balanced meal before starting their day. Kylie walked over and fixed herself a plate of eggs, bacon, and a biscuit. Then she got a glass of orange juice. As she was walking to a table to eat she saw her friend Amanda walking in.

"Kylie!" Amanda stopped as soon as she saw her. "You are in so much trouble. Head Cupid wants to see you in her office as soon as you get in today."

"Why? I didn't do anything wrong. She probably wants to tell me what a good job I did last night. I made a really awesome love connection last night."

"No." Amanda said. "She is very mad about something."

Kylie was nervous now. She had never been called into the office before. She wasn't sure what was going on.

"Mad. About what?"

"I don't know." Amanda said. "All I know is that she is not happy about something that happened last night."

Kylie walked on up the stairs and up to the boss' door. She thought it would be best not to drag it out. She rubbed her hands on her jeans and made sure her shirt was wrinkle free before knocking on the door.

"Come in," a voice that didn't sound too happy said from the other side.

Kylie walked in. "Ma'am. You wanted to see me?"

"Yes Kylie." Head Cupid said. "I am very upset about something you did last night."

"Why? All I did was make a love connection."

Head Cupid looked at Kylie with a stern look. She tossed the file down on her desk. "No! That is not all you did. You made a horrible mistake and a big mess of everything."

Kylie could feel her head spinning now. "What do you mean? I don't understand."

"Okay. Let's start from the beginning. What did you do?" Head Cupid said.

Kylie walked over and sat down in the chair. "I went to the restaurant last night. I saw a woman that looked sad that she was being stood up. It looked to me like it happened a lot. She kept looking at her phone, at a text. She looked sad. Then I saw a man come in and he looked lonely. So I thought why should she keep being treated like that and why should he be lonely? So I made a match. I put the two of them together. I made a love connection between the two of them. What did I do that was so wrong?"

Head Cupid walked over to her and patted her young cupid on the head. "Dear sweet girl. You can't always know what is going on in a person's life based on what you see on their face."

Kylie started to get tears in her eyes. She was feeling like maybe she had made a mistake. "What do you mean? What did I do?"

"Well the woman was not being stood up. Her boyfriend does indeed love her very much. He was texting her about some extremely bad news he had just received, which in turn made her sad. He was not standing her up. He was being held up due to a family member being rushed to the hospital. He had to go immediately to the hospital and could not go to dinner. The woman was upset because she wanted to be there for him and the family member and would have went right to him had you not stepped in when you did. And the man, he wasn't lonely. He was simply tired from a long day of working. His wife had to work late so he thought he would stop off and get some dinner before going home. He very much loves his wife. They have been together for ten years now."

Kylie stood up and started pacing back and forth. "Oh my. I've made such a horrible mistake. What am I going to do? I've ruined everything. I've made her in love with somebody else. She should be at the hospital with him but instead she is in love with another man. Oh no. I've ruined so many lives with my carelessness." She was crying uncontrollably now."

"Kylie you have to understand that these love connections are not made lightly. We put a lot of research into each case that we give to you. We don't go out and make connections on a whim. By changing one thing, it affects so many other things and so many other people. From now on you must follow all instructions moving forward."

Kylie was nodding her head. "Yes Ma'am. But how do I fix this?"

"I have corrected your mistake."

"What?" Kylie looked up. She wiped a tear away. "You fixed it?"

"I was watching everything and the mistake was corrected minutes after it was made. However, I may not always be there to fix your mistakes. You must remember that you can't make judgements based on what something looks like. You always do your research first. ”

Kylie walked over and gave her Head Cupid a hug. “Thank you so much for always being there for me.”

The End.

www.ingramcontent.com/pod-product-compliance
Lightning Source LLC
La Vergne TN
LVHW040957150826
845672LV00002B/729

9798230817468